Bit of a shock to be still here to be honest but it would appear that we've entered the new year unscathed. This edition of One Eye Grey was inspired in part by that most magic realist of things, the South London Press headline board. In particular the one last year that screamed 'ELEPHANT RATS ATTACK ICELAND' conjuring gorgeous images of giant be-tusked rodents assaulting that northern island and being fended off by divisions of Bjork commandoes. Of course it didn't take long to work out that what was really being said was that the Elephant and Castle outlet of a well known frozen food chain had something of a rodent problem.

That's South London for you promising wonders only to deliver rather less than that. Still we did once have a zoo in SE17 full of all manner of exotic species though probably not, in all honesty, elephant rats.
Our tales are not confined to one side of the Thames though as we take another visit to Chelsea, a first trip to West India Quay as well as Piccadilly, Kings Cross and other less easily identifiable locations for our stories from another London.

We are still looking for a few more tales for this year and to expand the number of outlets that stock One Eye Grey, which really takes up very little room. Far less than, say, a Russell Brand biography and without the attendant issue of people knocking it over whilst muttering 'prick' under their breath. Or, at least, not as much.

We should be back to bring some chill to the summer, though last year it was cold enough without us, with tales of the London skeleton, the second cellar, the terrifying birdman and much else beside including the truly awful Bank Holiday Weekend. Well aren't they all?

A STRANGE APPARITION IN CHELSEA

Unlike my Uncle Arnold, I never believed in spooks. He would often, after an especially good meal, leave a few titbits on his plate for 'hungry spectres', and claimed to be in regular contact with many of them. He even maintained that he had a formula to ward off the evil influence of spirits such as Putni, Ojha, Mambo, Massans and the Raksasis, all of them inveterate anthropophagi. On the other hand, he kept close friendships with many others, being particularly attached to a darling little spirit girl whom he often saw in Chelsea.

I was fond of him, and he was a very pious man, but I sometimes felt like laughing at his crazy ideas and visions, and feared that his eccentricities might cause him trouble. Late one night, I became somewhat impatient and exclaimed, 'What nonsense! There are no such things as ghosts!'

I could tell my uncle was hurt but he thought for a moment then replied, 'All right, Jim. I'll bet you £100 that I can convince you that ghosts exist.'

I laughed and agreed on the proviso that he told me where the little girl had come from, when she had lived in London, and why Chelsea. He smiled and told me to return in a month.

I could hardly wait and a month later we were again at table together. After a delicious meal, he left the wing of a chicken on his plate and settled back.

'Well, Jim,' he smiled benevolently. 'I've found the answer to all three of your questions but, as I know you won't believe me, you must go to the British Library and read a particular book there.'

He whispered a title in my ear and admonished me not to tell anyone else. He was as fond of his ghosts as some amateurs are of paintings they have stolen and hidden so that no one but themselves can look at them.

In the library, I obtained the book in question, which turned out to be an old leather-bound work in three volumes. Arnold, unfortunately (or deliberately), had not told me what part I was supposed to read, so I began wading through it. By the time I had perused half of it, having found nothing, I felt that the £100 was already in my pocket. Then, in volume two, I came across a passage about Ranelagh, Chelsea's famous Hanoverian Pleasure Gardens and its no less famous Rotunda.

Dr Johnson, who was never bored with London, described this as 'a place of innocent recreation'. All sorts of people spent agreeable evenings in its precincts. Noblemen rubbed shoulders with beggars, and royalty freely mixed with members of the English middle class. Fine, wigged young gentlemen became entangled in the crowd because they insisted on wearing their side swords. Beautiful, elegant ladies floated around like sailing boats in the gentle spring breeze in their wide-brimmed hats and flowing skirts, revealing tiny corners of petticoats trimmed with delicate lace frills. Crowds of people from all parts of the world! Among them were outlandish natives, including some children, as I could see from the sketch I had before my eyes. I looked at it and, as if struck by lightening, my heart skipped a beat. There before me were three Eskimos enjoying Ranelagh – a young man called Tugliavinia and his beautiful wife, Caubvic, with their four-year old daughter sitting in a wicker chair and smiling mischievously at me.

The author of the book had recorded (in English translation) a few Eskimo words that had been exchanged between the girl, whose name was Ikiyana, and a tall man of military appearance called George Cartwright. She had whimpered, 'Take me home' and he had replied, 'Yes, yes, I will,' in a soothing voice, to which her mother said, 'Thank you, George'.

A bit shaken, I hurried home and said to my wife, Jane:

'You don't mind. It's very important. We must go to Chelsea at once.' Everything had become astonishingly clear to me and even the date had a personal connection – 31st May – the anniversary of the death of my dear Labrador dog, Willy. It was another death that we needed to find out about then.

By the time we reached the other side of Chelsea Bridge it was 10.30 in the evening. I held my wife's arm nervously as we walked along the bank of the Thames. Suddenly, I saw what seemed to be a bundle of rags. It was so close that I could have touched it with my outstretched arms. I saw that it was a child but I did not believe that it was a ghost.

'Look', I turned to Jane.
'Where?' she asked.
'There in front of you.'

She replied that she could see nothing, which raised my hopes. Of course there was nothing there, I'd just imagined it. Then she carried on in a strange voice.

'You must be dreaming, George.'
I gasped with astonishment.
'Why do you call me George?' I muttered in a hoarse voice, trembling with emotion.
'What do you mean, Jim? I didn't call you George,' she retorted.

Now I understood everything. It was Ikiyana I had seen and, unwittingly, my wife had echoed Captain George Cartwright's soothing voice.

The next evening, I went to my uncle's house to eat humble pie and pay my wager, and to relate to him what I had seen and heard in Chelsea.

He listened to me, nodding approvingly from time to time. When I had finished my story, he said:

'Yes. Ikiyana is usually there at 11 o'clock, the time when she was at Ranelagh, but few people, except myself, ever see her. She died on 31st May 1772 while she was on her way home from England, and was interred on Mount Batten, a promontory at the south of Cattewater, a neck of land that helps to form the harbour of the Plymouth Estuary. She was buried by Captain George Cartwright in her sealskin dress, wrapped in a deerskin, together with her ornaments, sewing kit, and a knife and a spoon that she would need in the other world.

'Is there then a heaven for Eskimos?' I enquired.

'Indeed, there is. It's called Sedna, after an Eskimo goddess of the sea, and is situated six billion miles from Earth. It would take a space shuttle forty years to reach it. But,' he added, as the knowledgeable specialist that he is, 'it does not take so long for ghosts to cover the distance because they travel at more than a thousand times the speed of light. That's the only way a ghost living in the future can relive his or her past on earth.'

Then, pensively pursuing a train of thought all of his own, he declared in a solemn voice:

'It's an axiomatic truth among us "spectrologists" that ghosts are given one last chance to return to earth in order to settle a dispute or repay a debt to someone who has been very kind to them. Another of our axioms is that ghosts always return at a specific time, at a specific place, for a specific reason to a specific person. And she reappeared before you....'

'...to help you prove to me that ghosts do exist!' I ended his sentence.

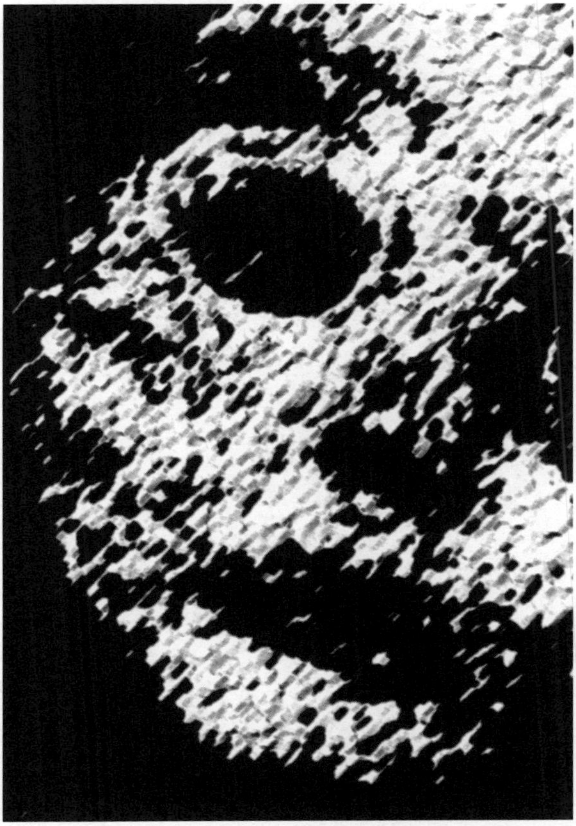

GENTS
from
atter of timing'
New York
STAN O'NEAL was last night fighting a
losing to save his Wall Street career,
as the of Merrill Lynch continued a
two- eting to decide the fate of the
bank battled chief executive.
O'Neal's position as chief executive
of the world's biggest invest ent bank
was severely damaged on Friday as it
was revealed he had held informal and
unauthorised merger talks with a rival.
News that the talks with Wachovia, a
big American banking group, were not
sanctioned by Merrill's board came just
days after O'Neal was forced to admit
that the value of debt-related
on the bank's
The combination of these two em
rassing blunders led to repeated
for O'Neal's immediate resigna
spokeswoman for O'Neal decli
comment, admitting only that
was in 'media silence' over the
Sources close to Merrill Lyn
however, that O'Neal had bee
board had lost confidence in
to lead and that his departure
a matter of timing'.
O'Neal's supporters insid
meanwhile, clung to the fac
no decision had been made
Larry Fink, founder and
Rock, the asset manageme
cent-owned by Merrill
Delta Two had to
backers this wee
£500m of workin
it had not allowed
sion-funding arra
investment pla
The revelation
down 3 per cent a
Sir Philip Hamp
panel for a dea
the takeover
n end to th
The Qa

The Newspaper Tycoon

'Once I was like you,' Norman sighed, resting his cigar stub in the ashtray. 'Hungry for work and no idea how I would find my way in the world.'

Paul moved his microphone closer, wondering if he should interrupt the old man's flow with a question. Sitting in the bar at the East India Club in St James's Square, he tried to picture Norman Clark, now in his eighties with his carved walking stick resting against his leather armchair, eating baked beans straight from a tin to save fuel.

This was Paul's first feature for The Times, and he wanted to make a big impression. Sharing a one-bedroom flat in Stockwell with a medical student was far from the dream that had led him to leave Liverpool. They had a rota for who slept in the bedroom and who got the sofa bed. Working twenty hours a week teaching English as a second language was about as glamorous as cutting toenails, and it only barely covered the rent.

He had sent an email to the features editor, suggesting an interview with Norman Clark, the reclusive owner of a group of newspapers, and had yelped with joy when he got an answer. Just one line, no capitals: '1200 wds on spec by end of week.' His godmother, Sally, the resident astrologer on one of Clark's papers, had suggested the assignment and helped him make contact with the tycoon. Okay, so it wasn't exactly a commission, but at least he hadn't been ignored and besides, what else would he be doing today? Reading a book at the lido?

'Is that thing on?' Norman asked, gesturing towards Paul's MiniDisk recorder. 'Don't want to have to repeat myself.' Paul checked. Yes, it was recording. Paul fumbled with the levels. If he could get the old boy to cough up a good story, maybe he'd be able to sell the interview to a radio station as well. 'Tell me how you got started,' he prompted.

Norman felt irritated that the reporter was recording the interview instead of taking it down in shorthand. No older than his grandson, he speculated, and probably just as feckless and lazy. Who had messed up the media? The press barons or Young Turks? Who had made it all so superficial?

'You probably think things weren't so difficult in the 'thirties, before women got it into their daft heads that they could interfere, before every half-wit with a laptop computer fancied himself as a writer, but actually it's never been easier. Especially for outsiders.'

'Outsiders?' Paul queried.

Norman raised his eyebrow. 'You know, foreigners. Aliens. What's the hip slang these days for a Yid? Kike? Clip-tip? Front wheel skid? Maybe you think that Jews are so well-connected that my path to Fleet Street was strewn with rose petals?'

Paul flushed, a little embarrassed. He had read that Norman had come from Vienna after the Anschluss in 1938, a teenage refugee. 'I'm sorry, do go on.'

Norman softened. 'My name in those days wasn't Norman, it was Siggy, Sigmund Kahn. My friends in Vienna called me Freud, but no one in London in those days was going to give a job to a cheeky chap called Siggy.

'It was a hot summer's day, just like today, and I didn't have a bean in my pocket. If you had told me then that one day I would have a chauffeur-driven Bentley and a wardrobe crammed with Savile Row suits, I would have split my sides laughing. I was sharing a room with another refugee who was working nights so I had to be out in the day while he slept. Anyway, one day I was busting for a piss but didn't look old enough to go into a public house, and had better manners than to relieve myself on the street.'

Paul couldn't see what this had to do with Norman's career as a newspaper proprietor, but from the faraway look on his face, the old man had gone back in time and Paul thought it better to let him ramble for a while. 'Where was that, sir?' asked Paul, deferentially.

'Piccadilly Circus, I recall. Just a few hundred yards from where we sit right now. Funny that, the clock has kept turning for the last sixty years and I've hardly moved from the same spot. Anyway, I saw a penny on the pavement and picked it up, pretending I was tying up my shoelaces. I headed straight for the nearest public convenience, the one next to the Eros statue. Maybe it's not there any more. Heaven knows I wouldn't go into one of those places these days, what with all those junkies and perverts and God knows what other troglodytes. Where was I? Oh yes, by amazing luck, one of the toilet doors was opened, so I had my pee and still had my penny as well.'

This was not the rags-to-riches story Paul had anticipated. He was vaguely starting to regret having followed his godmother's advice. If he wanted to work regularly with The Times, this interview would have to be an ace of spades, not a joker.

'With that penny, I bought some pencils from the market, and took them down to Ludgate Circus, where I sold them for a nice profit to journalists rushing to work, and then bought some more. The following week I added notepads and erasers to my wares and set up a little stall. I enrolled in an evening class in English and another in shorthand and started jotting down some stories myself. One day, one of my regular clients took the trouble to ask me a bit about myself, where I was from, what I wanted to do, that sort of thing. I showed him one of my articles. A piece about the bowler hat. He asked if he could show it to his editor and they gave me a job. Not writing at first, of course, but making tea. And I brewed the best tea any hack has ever drunk, weird though I thought it was in those days that you Brits put milk in your tea. Where I come from, you only drink milky tea when you're sick.

'The thing is, son, I didn't have anything to lose, and since my roommate was out every night, I figured I needed to improve my lot more than I needed the sleep, so I spent those hours writing up little vignettes about British life and eventually one of them got published. But I hadn't forgotten my lesson about the pencils and knew that to get out of that vulnerable situation, I had to start a newspaper myself. The Fleet Street Messenger, I called it. I wrote under several pseudonyms and sold copies myself outside St Paul's station. Amazingly, I sold out of every copy from that first print run. I invited readers' contributions and published those too, in the next issue.'

Norman paused while he drew on his cigar. Paul was now listening attentively. This was more like it. He wondered if Sally knew Norman's story and had sent him on this mission for an existential lesson on how to get on in life.

'I bet you'd like to thank whoever dropped that penny.'

'No,' said Norman. 'The man I'd like to thank is the one who left the toilet door open.'

When I see an Elephant Fly

Sunday morning and I was yawning. Also, the cat was bouncing around aggressively, shouting his demands for goods and services, most specifically his breakfast and the opening of windows at the front so he could do his park inspection and show off on the window ledge.

Before I met the animal's food needs, it was time for a retrospective on the previous night. I always found the trip up to Primrose Hill vexing and I shouldn't have bothered going at all, really. I'd never liked that side of my family, with their smug other-worldliness, although I might have had a bit of that if I'd walked their streets. As it stood, my other worlds had to be reached by more temporal means. My head was throbbing. Whatever had been in that gear had clearly been smuggled in from another planet. Pluto would have been my best guess. At Primrose Hill, I'd pleaded poverty, danger and an early appointment, nipped through the fragrant streets to Chalk Farm tube and taken the dark shunter south to Kennington. Almost certainly, there had been a conversation after I'd left, along the lines of:

'Poor Carl. But best not to be too late on those streets.'
'Why didn't he get a taxi?'
'Will they go south at this time?'
'Now, now. Kennington's not so bad, I hear.'

'Well, maybe not. But he lives on one of the estates in Walworth. As he says, the nearest tube doesn't always indicate where you live and giving your tube name as a means of stating locale is just a north London conceit. Mind you... do you say you live in Chalk Farm or Primrose Hill?'

'Walworth? Really? How brave!' This would be Octavia, the most palatable of the bunch. 'I heard it's rough as a fighting otter down there.'

The rest would have smiled at that and their conversation would then have turned to happier topics.

I, of course, was not brave, and not too poor or unable to get a taxi. But you judge your evenings by their potential outcomes and last night was definitely no occasion to stay beyond the last tube. Kennington was great, too, because all trains stopped there. Unlike, say, Chalk Farm.

Once back on the sunny side, I strode through what my family no doubt regarded as the mean streets of SE17. In reality, the meanest thing about the area was people's opinion of it, but I was about to enter one of the only really rough places in it by choice. And I was only about to enter The Giraffe pub because I needed some sanity after the transpontine yap I'd been hearing for the last couple of hours. The Giraffe, or The Long Neck, as some affectionately called it, was less a public house and more a gin palace with an apothecary sideline. Or a pharmacy that sold beer. The long-abandoned pool table mostly served as a handy surface for cutting up weights on, and its cue sticks and balls had all been used up in rumbles over the years.

The pub got its name from the fact that, in the long ago and far away, the first giraffe to arrive in the UK was landed from the canal that once ran through what is now Burgess Park. The beast was allowed to wander the neighbourhood for a while, before it was exhibited in Surrey Zoological Gardens, which once stretched from the site of the council dump and old baths on Manor Place, and across Lorrimore Common as far as Kennington Park Road, just south of the tube. According to legend, the extension to the back of The Giraffe pub had been constructed from stones recycled from the old zoo entrance at Manor Place. Next to the zoo had been the home of the Surrey County Cricket Club, before it moved to nearby Oval. I loved the idea of men in sportswear, clutching their cricket bats and strolling through SE17, the sounds and smells of the wildlife of Asia and Africa and Latin America all around them.

Of course, we still had all of that today, but in a different way and the only wildlife of note were the foxes, cats, pigeons and dogs. In complexion, features, manners and behaviour, these creatures were replicated inside the Long Neck. At least, they were if you were an aspirant seventies comedian and, sadly, many of the clientele harboured ambitions in that direction.

'You see, Carl, you've got your sharp-faced foxes, your busty vixens, some sweet pussy, a few old birds and a couple of dogs,' one of the resident wags just back from a short stay at the Windsor chain of hotels once informed me. Aside from the animals, all of humanity was here, or at least, most of its dark side.

I ordered a cider and looked around for Biffa the herbalist, while instinctively moving away from Scrubba and Washa. Scrubba had once been a graffiti artist of some note, before spending a few years on the brown. And cider and white had done for Washa's ambitions (fortified by a cultural studies degree from South Bank Polytechnic) to be a television presenter. In the British fashion, Washa was so called because she didn't, and Scrubba's name derived from some long-forgotten soft drink commercial. It must have been a very long time ago, because I couldn't possibly associate Scrubba with a soft drink of any description.

I found Biffa and bought a few sticks' worth of something he assured me was top quality, to go with my pint. Sipping on one and sparking the other, I looked over the premises.

The Giraffe had all the qualities of an estate pub. Multi-racial yet clannish, full of great beauty and tremendously sexy, yet unremittingly ugly at the same time, awash with flaring hope and studied despair. At least, that's how my friends from the north might have seen it, once they got over the initial shock that the only food served were nuts and

Wotsits. The only customers too, come to that.

I was quite happy only to be an irregular visitor. There were a couple of sorts at the bar, one of whom, Lily, I vaguely knew from the neighbourhood and the odd night in the pub. She'd distinguished herself on one occasion by the use of, possibility the last, pool cue to batter a bloke who had two-timed her friend Michelle.

'Where you been tonight then?' Bright eyes, tight top, tough pretty face.
'Primrose Hill.'
'What's that like. Any good?' Checking out the area around her.
'OK. Bit up itself.'
'Yeah, I heard that. We're off to Dingles later.' The night was really only just starting.

'I heard that'd been taken over.' And so we drifted into comparisons of the merits and demerits of a selection of local venues, before the inevitable interruption.

The rattle, when it came, did not arrive from a clear blue sky. Nothing could ever be said to be really clear here. The weather was permanently changeable, with each gust from the door potentially brewing up a storm. The trick was to know what might blow over and what would blow up.

Lily, with her native intuition, nodded to her confederates, touched my hand and suggested we all exit sharpish. She pulled me through the portal that led out the back to the rear of George's the newsagents, and said, 'That was close. It was about to get very lairy in there.'

We looked at each other for a while and I was struck just how fantastically turned out Lily and her mates were. I thanked her for the tip-off and headed for home, a couple of minutes' walk away. I reflected that it is never too early to leave the Giraffe. There were strange smells and sounds as I turned the corner into Amelia Street and

I attributed these to the drains, which often backed up. And the lingering effects of the bob I'd smoked.

As I was groggily piecing these reminiscences together, I became conscious of a different kind of beast making his presence known with great insistence. Reluctantly, I got up, staggered into the kitchen, put on the kettle, fed the cat, then, tea in hand wandered to the front room to open the window for him. Looking out at the park opposite, I was startled to see that it appeared to have grown overnight. Across the road was the same attractive arrangement of shrubs and benches but beyond the pathway the estate had vanished. Now, there was just an open expanse of grassland and, past that, a sign proudly announcing the Royal Surrey Zoological Garden. I fancied that over the top of one of the fences I could see a giraffe.

What had been in that gear?

Absent-mindedly, I picked up a paper lying on my coffee table. It was a stylishly presented thing called Walpaper – 'The paper for London's most fashionable borough'. The headlines screamed 'Lofty Ambitions: Living the high life by the canal in Burgess Village'; 'Walworth Worthies oppose fast-food application on High Street' ('Out of character with the area, claims local MP Peter Tatchell'). Inside, it promised the latest on the Elephant redevelopment and the appearance of Salman Rushdie at a local bookshop event. I opened it to the centre pages, where there was a special feature on the celebrity clusters within Wonderful Walworth.

I was clearly dreaming. But on inspecting the article, I was delighted to note that broadcast media heavyweights favoured Sutherland Square, while West Camberwell was the place for the arty mob. Heygate Heights attracted the city types and the literary set could be found between Browning Street and Liverpool Grove either side of the fashionable souk of East Street, with its parade of designer shops. Stella McCartney had a flat on the canal, Albany Road was favoured by the music industry and a clutch of film stars lived just south of the zoo between Kennington Common and the Brandon Village. The phone interrupted my learning about parallel-Walworth. It was Octavia.

'Carl, oh I'm glad you're in. I wondered if we could drop by later. I promised the children a trip to the zoo and you know how they love the view from your roof.'

I muttered something vaguely positive.
'They were so excited about seeing Daniel Radcliffe last time,' continued Octavia.
I said I'd love to see them.
'Oh you are good, you can't imagine how nice it is to get off the hill and into somewhere civilised. There was another stabbing last night on Adelaide Road, it's the third this month. And Alfred couldn't get a taxi from the West End last week unless he paid the driver in advance.'

'That's shocking,' I said. Without thinking, I added, 'Shall I meet you at the tube? We could go to the zoo that way.'

'Oh, yes. And maybe we could go to the canal later. You're so lucky living in such a beautiful part of the city.'

I concurred, eyeing as I did what looked like a rather elegant café next to the railway, which, in my memory, had been the home of an ugly training centre for the unemployable. Let them serve cake, I mused. Or buns for the elephants.

On the way to the tube, I met fair-trader in coffee, Biffah, returning from his jog. Further off, I could see E'Screwbar and Wah Shah strolling arm-in-arm.

Biffah grinned at me and said, 'I'd avoid those two if I were you. He's been offered half a million for his next book and she's going to be on the Late Cultural Review as co-presenter. Ran into them at Cou Long last night, couldn't get away. They kept going on about a north city cultural tour they'd been on. Honestly, you'd think it was Baghdad, the way they were talking. I mean it can't be that bad can it? You've got family there, after all.'

I nodded, and he carried on.

'They'd been up at the site of Watkin's Tower. Apparently, the rebuild is way over budget. But one thing they did tell me that was quite funny – there used to be a zoo up in NW1. Nearly as popular as ours, but when the royal family shifted their animals from the Tower, they gave them to us, along with a subsidy, and that tipped the balance. The north London zoo closed and that was when the area began to sink into poverty.'

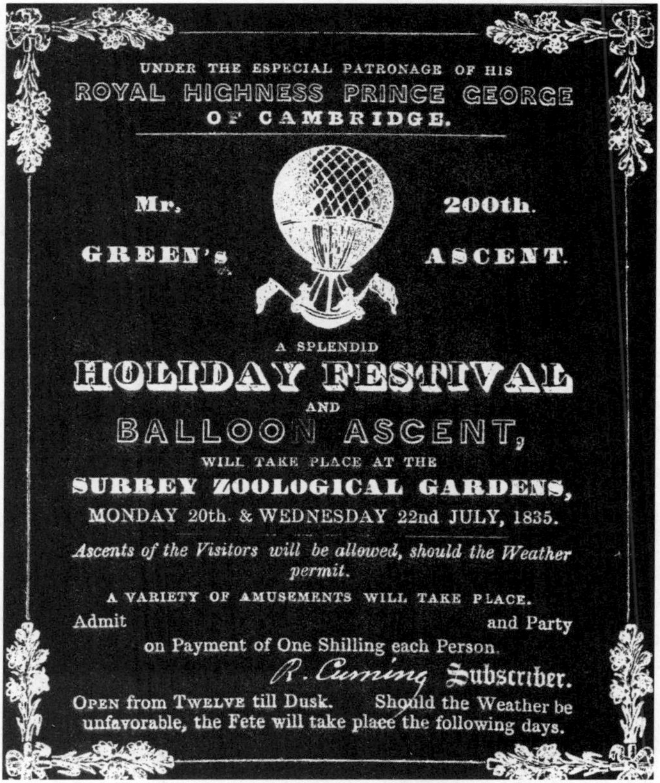

ATLANTIC ROAD
SW
CCTV
IN OPERATION
MAKING BRIXTON
A SAFER PLACE

Atlantic Road

Clouds pass over the hard sunlight, a good sign that the rain and thunder has passed over us. The red brick and black tarmac in which the house nestles is warming up and drying off.

'Good light for photography,' says Martin.

Simon, Helen and I, are in the living room; the blinds are, as ever, half-drawn and I'm sunk in my regular trough on the sofa near Helen, bantering to get in the mood for another drug adventure.

I watch Strange Martin getting ready to go out for another day's photography.

'Digital camera,' he mutters to himself. 'Old camera. Film, film, film, film. Boots. Combats with lots of pockets.'

'Down Atlantic Road, mate,' Simon is saying, waving a bag, 'there's this bloke, not your usual sort, grey skin and got a face like he's had a stroke, like stuck. I was on the look out for some weed and I got these instead.'

'He, what, just gave them to you?' asks Helen.

'Yeah, for free. I didn't know what to do with 'em but I saw Vinny and he said they were "mental gear" and...'

'Vinny?' I ask.

'Yeah, well,' Simon folds his face into a grin, 'well, the Camberwell squat-lot too, they said it's got great visuals or something.'

'Vinny?' glares Helen.

'Look, do you want to try these things or not?'

Helen looks to me, I nod. Martin hasn't left yet.

'Martin. How're you?'

'Yeah, not bad, going out to photograph some stuff.'

'Bomb sites? Train crash spots again?'

He gives me a look like he's above me, like walking to places where horrible things have happened to people and photographing them is some great form of sodding art.

'I don't need drugs to make life interesting or scary. I have my eyes,' says Martin. Then his eyes mist over, like they do sometimes. 'You know when you take ice from the freezer and a trail of cold mist follows it? Or you lift a chalky rock and dust floats around it? The pills have that: some part is hovering around them waiting for them to be taken.'

Then he walks out, no doubt satisfied with his latest strange thing. He goes off to whatever adventure he's got in store for himself and we, pills in hand, go off on ours.

My eyes drop to the floor and don't stop. Everything goes a reddish black then my mind, my vision, emerges somewhere else. It's like being in the middle of something, not just a weird feeling and vision: Don't think, a voice says. Let us in and let go.

Go with the fleshy sphere falling through a forest canopy, I'm crashing through purple and mauve leaves, through air that's warm and thick and rolls aside as I fall. I hit the ground and burst, scattering innards that grow roots that carry on downwards and lose themselves in the darkness of the soil.

An explosion that stretches across millions of miles of cold darkness; I have swung through space for countless years and now I have met, for the first time ever, something like myself. A belt of blue gas merges with my own, now billowing, gold. The blue buckles and breaks into tornados and spherical whirlpools that grow white-hot and heavy as we pass through each other.

I am a piece of meat, a severed head, I feel my brains, skull, flesh, the scaly plates of my skin, the wound that separates me from my body and the tip of the cobalt growth like a pyramid that pushes into that wound. There is no horror in these but a peace. I feel the mineral I am impaled upon vibrate and sing as it starts to break my molecules, bone, blood, thoughts and my self down, and draw them in.

I roll with two rutting clouds, I am warm, the other is hard and cold and we collide, casting sparks of thunder to the ground. I ride down with the lightning that blasts through a tree's core. The tree splits and hisses and I am back on earth again.

I can feel where I am, still on the sofa, Helen nearby and Simon opening his eyes.

'That was something,' Simon says. 'I'm not totally sure what, but it was a thing. How about you chaps?'

Everything looks wrong. Well... feels wrong. I know that I've been in this dirty house, mostly on this sofa, for ages but I've absolutely no idea why. My head churns with alien things far more vital than this dust-clogged room.

'Yeah, I'm ok,' says Helen, 'I'm not sure that all the stuff that went through my head was me, but no lasting damage, I don't think.'

'Nat, you ok?' she asks me.

There's a light in her eyes that I don't recognise, something fierce and possessive and strong. The light reaches toward me. Something has happened and I don't think I should stay here. I mumble that I have to go. The worlds in my head mean more than this room or the light in her eyes.

Atlantic Road smells real enough; scorched oil, ripe fruit, crushed vegetables and blood-soaked sawdust. The railway arches are where all the wiry blokes and girls in their greasy headwear gather.

There had been something powerful in Helen's eyes as she spoke to me: a light that reached out toward me.

Those alien things I'd seen after I took the tablet weren't like a trip. Trips are your own world screwed up with chemicals that occasionally invite the creatures from your subconscious out to play. I was the severed head. I'd felt the cold of the other cloud as we collided and pushed lightning out between us. I'd felt nebulas meet, merge and collide to make something new. These had come from creatures that were not my own. Now, all I know is that this world - Brixton, that room, Helen, Simon - is not real.

The grey man emerges from the wall. Simon was right: face, clothes, the flat, thick hair, it's all grey and the face is frozen. No real eyes, just a bulge and a white patch, as if the detail of moving eyes is too much to create.

Whatever it is, this is a convenient form for it to have, to pass on its pills. And as I think the word, a hand without fingernails drops a pill into my hand. After the delivery, the apparition blinks out of sight and I'm left with the pill, its seething aura and a great need to take it.

The only place I can think to go is Brockwell Park. There, I place myself under a dying tree; all yellowing leaves and the scent of scorched wood. The pill goes in, my stomach bristles and accepts it and I'm going out there again. This time, though, I know what I'm getting.

I'm a mass of greasy orange fur, teeth and yowling and scowling in the middle of a street. The small, aching fox mind I'm in knows of nothing except the urgency of the sex but my own mind can see this is a flash into something, an act of creation. I spot the pot holes and patterns of cracked paint on the doors of SW9's Railton Road. I hear the thunder and feel the burst of rain. This happened last night and somehow I'm remembering it, not the fox.

I recognise the sharp chilli and thick chocolate taste of the air at the Columbian café in Brixton Market. In the air is the story of a girl at a party, snogging a bloke who disappears halfway through a kiss.

'She was wrecked,' the mouth says, 'but she didn't know she was so wrecked it'd take her five minutes to realise he'd gone.'

I follow the anecdote to the ear of the listener, changing from sound to whatever nebulous entity a thought is. I feel the story in the first head and I feel it bend and buckle to fit the head it has arrived in; it has split and anticipates changing and spreading further with each re-telling.

The story has a life of its own, even beyond the event, and it urges the tellers to retell it so it can spread - it's as randy as a fox. Story and memory are an expanding country of their own.

I'm elsewhere. I'm dry, my flesh and bones are fused. My dreams and thoughts are still with me: quicksilver movement in cold, wide seas, the feeling of water flowing through me. The bodies and ghosts of my brothers and sisters whisper with me; the memory of sunbeams piercing the ocean is shared with me from my nearest brother as he takes the memory of coasting along a warm current from me. These recollections fade as we lie there together: dead but remembering. Then a bell rings and the ghosts take flight somewhere I cannot follow, leaving me with the knowledge that ghosts fear the ringing of bells.

I recognise it now, though. It's a counter-bell in one of the stalls inside Brixton Market, it gets the bloke who runs the shop to stop watching his little portable telly and serve someone with the giant snails and dried fish he sells there. I'm more aware this time, perhaps because the visions aren't gathered from such alien places this time.

Stories started in Brixton cafes, memories shared by fading souls, suns created a billion light-years from here, something new growing from a severed head and a cobalt blue mineral. I am these things, briefly, and in seeing them I lose something of my own. At first, I think these bright and alien visions make my own life look pointless, but that isn't it. Memory and story are living things that have parasites, things that travel for light-years searching for new lands to occupy. Simon was wrong: those pills do have a price. Memories are collected by something, something that has asked to be let into my head. It has taken something from me - a memory. And the loss of that memory has made my world meaningless.

It's dark, there's something, someone, warm against me and we're both moving. My heart is punching the inside of my ribcage, flushing hot blood through me. I feel a bra strap under one hand, nylon pulled away from soft skin, and I open my eyes. Helen is there with me, we're in the living room, tiny lines of sun shining through the dusty old blinds, tangled together on the sofa, pulling each other's clothes off. It is the day we get the sofa into our house, we're hot, tired, and suddenly realise there is something between us. There's a light in her eye that is also in mine, another living thing without physical presence but more real than anything.

That piece of myself returns to me, as stolen memories of other worlds fade forever and I can go home.

MIRACLES · HEALING · FAITH
MICHAEL REID MINISTRIES
SEE WHAT GOD CAN DO FOR YOU

The Deadwoods Song

He thought it was foxes at first. Off in those woods at night. He knew from previous experience that they sounded like murder victims when they copulated. And it was that time of year. Cold, sharp February nights. The sound cutting through the dark as he lay in bed, drifting off. Distant and indistinct at first. He was able to dismiss it almost immediately and slip anchor into sleep's safe waters.

But one night, it started a bit earlier. He could hear it above the TV. Put it on mute, paused, listening. It came again, still distant, but it carried and cut through the air. It was unlike any fox he'd ever heard. It was not a sound of back gardens and alleyways. Deep inside, he felt something un-nameable stirring, ready to clutch his innards with a dread hand. But the sound died off, and he went to bed, deciding to forget all about it. Which he did. Until it woke him two nights later as he dozed in the armchair. This time, it sounded more intense and closer. Intermittent, distorted, frequently buried beneath the sound of the evening's last pulse of traffic. But it was there all the same. It was impossible to pinpoint the source as he stood, scalp prickling, window open, ears straining. Impossible to pinpoint, except he knew it was in those woods.

During the summer that followed, there was just an occasional reminder on the odd night, just after dark. Once, he thought he heard something right outside the building when he got up, a horrible moment that froze his innards before he realised it must have been cats fighting. Gradually, he shrugged off the creeping unease; gradually, things returned to normal and he continued with his solitary life just as he'd always done.

But then, as the autumn days shrank to withered remnants, it came back with a vengeance, waking him the small hours, in the quiet time between 1am and 3am when the city pauses in statis. The dead hours, when he was acutely aware of just how alone he was, with only a hollow honeycomb of cold rooms around and above him. He almost wished for the oblique comfort of the departed insomniac upstairs, whose creaking boards and shuffling sounds had at least been evidence of normal life.

He tried to explain the sound away. But it was getting louder, still indistinct but like the memory of a voice. It was definitely out there and not in his head. Out there. Someone screaming. And after a week, it was no longer alone. One Friday, he jolted awake at 2.40am and, frozen in the dark, realised there was a second and a third voice joining the scream. Garbled shouts, laced with animal fear, weird and intermittent, as if emanating from a detuned radio or snatched up and carried off by a capricious wind.

But then back again, just that bit closer every time. He lay, heart in mouth, clutching the duvet to himself, limbs locked, reduced to a child again. Then, abruptly, the sounds died off, flickered and failed. He lay awake for another hour, staring at the ceiling, listening. Listening.

Listening.

But the woods stayed silent. And eventually he found sleep once more, just half an hour before the alarm went off.

There were better nights and bad nights but he found himself constantly listening out, just the same. From the time he walked home from the station – now always on the side of the road furthest from the trees – and all through his routine until bed. While he cooked. As he sat in the lounge, TV turned low. He stopped playing music because he became convinced that every time a song began the voices started up outside, and he could hear them just beneath the sounds from the speakers.

He couldn't remember his dreams but he sensed they had been taken over by something unspeakable. Around the anniversary of his first killing, it started getting worse. The sounds were now unmistakable: it was a fluctuating chorus of human cries. Cries of pain. Of fear. Of terrible suffering, in the different keys of men, women, children, some so garbled and unspeakably horrible they were beyond defining. They rose and fell, sometimes a lone voice, sometimes what sounded like ten or more, ebbing and flowing like some dark estuarine tide, rich with the silt of human suffering, flowing up out of those woods in the small dead hours when the city slowed and slept. The sounds were beyond ignorable – they cut to the marrow. He knew that nobody else could hear them; no lights ever flicked on in the other flats, no blinds or curtains ever stirred during those episodes. No police cars were ever called. He was more alone than ever. He began to recognise some of the cries out there on the derelict city air, among the chokes, the pleas for mercy and the fucking awful, awful screams. He recognised them as the voices of the men he'd murdered. The same pleas, the same screams, broadcast on repeat as if the very air had recorded them.

His nights became an ordeal. For most of the week, a tatty Tantalus promise of sleep was held out, dangled cruelly just beyond reach. The chorus made sure of that. He tried sleeping in different rooms, as far from the windows as possible. But the sounds followed him wherever he chose to barricade himself. He tried sleeping tablets but they worked only intermittently. He tried drink, but he couldn't get used to the taste, even in tea, and it just made him sick before he could render himself insensible.

It seemed as if the voices knew he was attempting to cheat them, to shut them out, and they increased their assault accordingly. The lack of sleep quickly eroded him, stripped his days of reason. His timekeeping grew erratic; he lost weight, his health plummeted. People at work commented. His head of section, Myers, called him in for a meeting, feigning concern, delivering veiled disciplinary threats. He stopped going to work. He fell behind on the rent. He had the money in the bank to cover it but his grasp on the rituals of order and routine had slipped. He'd fallen into a place that imprisoned him.

And then one evening, just before Christmas, after three days without real sleep, he drifted off through sheer exhaustion. After a while, the empty black void gave way to a vision. The first man he'd killed came to him in this dream. The man's face looked different in proper light, somehow, though it was still intact, like it had been before the hammer blows. Except he had the same glasses on, and one lens was a spider's web of cracked glass. He also wore the same overcoat, now crusted with patches of leaves and mud, and something else that was dark, around the lapels and down the front.

The man in the dream was in his kitchen, boiling the kettle, which wouldn't switch off so the steam was steadily filling the room, condensing on the tiles and window. The man turned and looked at him with an unreadable expression, and then he smiled in a sad, melancholy way. Smiled at the night-sweat fear and confusion smeared across his murderer's face.

'You still don't know what's happening, do you?' The dead man asked quietly, but his voice was clear above the agitated tumult of boiling water, as if he'd been standing right next to him in the doorway.

'They're coming to you,' he said. 'All of them. The dead of this city, all the murdered dead. They hear our voices in your woods, they find them and they join them. And there are so many of us now.'

'I don't want this, I didn't mean for this to happen, for any of it. I don't want them here, please. Please. Please.' The smile faded from the dead man's face. A pause, like molasses, like the thickening blood so fastidiously scrubbed away each time; the blood of four dead men. Slow and heavy, time pregnant with a sickly pressure. Then the man spoke again.

'And you think I can stop it, do you? That's not possible now. You've started something. And me? Well, I'm part of it.'

He woke himself up, drenched in the sharp-smelling sweat of the stranger he'd become. He screamed at the ceiling, imploring his invisible neighbours: 'Can't any of you hear them? What's wrong with you all?'

He fell back on the sofa in the dark, gasping for breath, crying. Silence now, except the purr of the refrigerator, the regular soft click of the smoke alarm system. A moment of normality and he felt himself edging towards the steadying hand of calm, heart rate diminishing, the safe reality of his old life grasped, welcomed back with tearful gratitude once again. All just a nightmare. And then he heard a click, as someone switched on the kettle in the kitchen.

As if on cue, the voices started again in the woods. Only now they weren't just out there in the dark across the road. There were more of them in the front garden, on that impeccably manicured lawn beneath the lounge window. Louder now, closer. More of them, trailing footprints of mud, leaf mould and blood. He knew they'd be standing on the lawn, their ruined faces raised to his windows like grotesque parodies of carol singers, their mouths open ovals of eternal night. Endlessly repeating their inarticulate dying cries. Their screams, their curses, their pleas – a discordant, dissonant choir of human suffering, forever trapped. The women, beaten, violated and killed by predatory rapists and enraged ex-boyfriends. The children, abducted and strangled on cold waste ground and in darkened garages. The vagrants and prostitutes who'd fallen through society and disappeared without leaving a single fingerprint on life. And the suicides, driven to ultimate despair by a life they could not escape and could no longer bear. A black wave of sound endlessly breaking against him; a chorus of the night beyond night, meant only for his ears.

And he couldn't block it out anymore. It was a terrible music he would only be free of when he joined them. He threw his head back, opened his throat, and started to scream back at them. And once he'd started, he found he couldn't stop.

Harlots!

The Thrash

Penny and Jenny. It was probably inevitable that they would pair up – Cockneys like rhymes. Often, Cockney girls who work on the edge of Canary Wharf also like ambitious cockney boys who work in big financial institutions, and the place they called the Castle was full of them on a Friday night. Penny and Jenny liked to be bought champagne until the bar shut, following which Penny and Jenny would split up, go home with the men they'd chosen and meet up again at lunchtime at a pub in Poplar to giggle and gossip about what they'd been up to, before heading to clothes shops to try, unsuccessfully, to replicate the clothes worn by the Canary Wharf women.

Until the smoking ban, they'd head to the Castle's loos together at regular intervals to discuss tactics but now they did this outside. Leaving a group of office workers to discuss whatever office workers discussed – Penny and Jenny worked in shops on Bow Market – they lit up outside the Castle and walked around the side of the long row of bars and restaurants so as not to be overheard.

'Whaddya think of Dale?' asked Penny. Jenny shrugged.

'Seems more interested in that stuck up tart with the fringe. One of the Darrens is eyeing you up, you know.'

Penny faked a gasp.

'Which one?'

Jenny was about to answer, but instead, screamed. Penny looked over her shoulder and this time her gasp wasn't fake. Jenny was grasping her backside and swearing. Penny couldn't believe her eyes.

Standing behind Jenny was a figure dressed in old-fashioned clothes – she couldn't judge the period – wielding a whip.

'Harlots!' shouted the figure and, with an expert flick of the whip, managed to make the whip lash out beyond Jenny and wrap itself painfully around Penny's behind.

'He's cut my fucking arse!' shouted Jenny as Penny began to scream.

People began running to where the two girls were sobbing and swearing. The whip had cut through their short skirts and cut deeper. Jenny was bleeding.

'What happened?' asked the first person to arrive. The girls turned to point at the shadowy figure that had assaulted them, but he was nowhere to be seen.

James looked out over the empty bar that regulars had nicknamed the Castle, although the regulars didn't come in now. The name had come from some of the bar's features. It belonged to a chain of pubs that had experimented with themed bars at the end of the 1990s. A few had been given a mediaeval theme, including this one. It hadn't caught on and the staff no longer had to wear tabards, but the company was too mean to remove the fittings, so the fake portcullis and battlements remained. Unlike the regulars.

A mobile buzzed and James answered.

'No, Frank, no-one. Come over and cheer me up, will you? OK.'

He hit the end-call button and sighed. The last few customers he'd had were reporters. None of them had taken the assaults seriously – there had been more than ten now – and puns and cartoons were about all they'd had to offer until the Standard printed a close-up of one of the wounds. Then the broadsheets had picked up on it, and then – nothing.

The police were baffled, not one woman had been able to describe her assailant, beyond the fact that he was wearing antique clothing. And although only two more of the victims had actually been drinking in the Castle, the press had linked the pub to the attacks, so no woman would come near and thus no man would either. Even the gay ones.

James stood near the front of the bar, idly wiping tables that hadn't been used since the last time he'd wiped them, watching the Thursday night crowds walk over the bridge from Canary Wharf and turning left. Never right. Never to the Castle. Except one – Frank.

'How's it going then?' said Frank. He was a big, ebullient man who represented the chain and spent most of his time visiting the pubs and bars they owned for various reasons. A troubleshooter, that's what he called himself. A busybody, that's what the successful managers called him. James hoped he would be a lifesaver.

They sat in the otherwise empty bar and James explained the situation.

'Well, there's nothing you can do to make the public stop thinking of this place as part of the problem. Not unless they catch this nutter. But I do have an idea.' Frank picked up his mobile.

'Hi, it's Frank. Are any of the vampire crew there yet? Get one of the organisers over, will you?' James stared at him. Frank covered the mouthpiece and whispered, 'Marlborough Head'.

James understood, but was perplexed. A group of vampire fans met regularly at the Marlborough, a horror-themed pub that had retained its décor. What that had to do with his problem he didn't know.

The figure on the quay outside was attracting attention, and this was hardly surprising. He was dressed in Victorian clothing, almost all of it black or scarlet. He was also, apparently angry. He entered the Castle.

There were only a couple of photographers there, but Giles had insisted they made sure the bar was full, as it had been when the first attack took place. He needed the photographers inside because his stunt (as Frank called it) or exorcism (as Giles called it) had to be unseen. More or less.

Penitentia and Januaria were not their real names. Their short, tight leather skirts covered spiderweb tights and were reinforced beneath by leather knickers. Their Victorian-style bodices were revealing and their demands on Frank and James insistent. Giles had talked them into coming along the previous night, promising cash, and they had gone out of their way to be here. Frank sighed and was paying them half up front when there was a commotion outside.

A figure in antique clothes was being dragged away by the police. There was a rush for the door, as pressmen and photojournalists tried to be first on the scene.

James grinned. An actual flesh and blood pervert had been arrested and his bar could start making money again.

'Might as well go home ladies. Giles, it seems it's all...'

'But he was with me!' said Frank. The four people left in the bar turned towards him.

'I thought if you did this exorcism, he could jump out,' he said. 'Then he was supposed to drive off. There's a car round the back. Thought it might do the trick...'

Giles frowned.

'Carry on, girls,' he said.

'I've been stopped three times by police and searched for a bloody whip. I'm missing the vampire meet and I've had about a dozen girls run away from me. This had better be worth it.'

Frank leaned over the counter and grabbed some notes from the float in the till.

'£50 do you?'

The ageing goth, whose name was Giles, took the money eagerly.

'For now. So, you want to know what to do about the ghost of Whipping Jack, do you?'

'Who?' asked James and Frank simultaneously. Giles smiled.

'In the late 18th century, someone began whipping women's bottoms at random, in the streets of this part of London. He was nicknamed Whipping Jack. He was never caught. After the crimes of Jack the Ripper a century later, he was forgotten. Seems to me like he's back.'

James turned to Frank.

'What's this all about?'

'Look, we can't stop the public associating this place with this Whipping Jack character,' said Frank. 'So lets get it associated with a solution. Now I don't believe in ghosts, but we need publicity. Is there anything you can do, Giles? Something the press would be interested in?'

The mysterious stranger smiled.

'Well, you can give me the cab fare back to central London. I've got an idea.'

Penitentia and Januaria shrugged. Frank tried to make his way outside to explain what had happened, but he was blocked by the horde of pressmen. James watched Giles, who had taken a seat at a table, his back to the area where the first attack had taken place, and was mumbling something. The two women began walking to the side area where Penny and Jenny were assaulted.

What happened next was never clear to James. He didn't see where the tall, night-black figure came from, he just saw him, it – or whatever – lash out. Januaria was hit squarely on her buttocks. She reacted instantly, turning away from the dark shape and saying, 'Mmm. Do it again'.

Penitentia turned away too, stuck her leather-clad nether regions out provocatively and said, 'No, me next, me next!'

'Harlots!' shouted the figure, lashing out at Penitentia.

'Come on, do it again,' said Januaria. But she was speaking to empty air.

By then the press were there, but it was too late. Penitentia and Januaria were immediately snapped by photographers, showing off the cuts in their dresses and a lot more. Giles grinned and entered the bar.

James followed.

'What just happened?'

'Well… when a ghost appears in order to punish the wicked, it spoils things if the wicked enjoy the punishment. Penitentia and Januaria are regulars at Torture Garden, they could have taken a lot more and still enjoyed it. I think your problems are over.'

And so it proved. The press picked up on the name Whipping Jack for a while, then forgot the incident. Penitentia and Januaria both got a little modelling work and a brief spot as agony aunts on one of the instant-litter commuter rags. Giles got to host a six-part series on a documentary channel so obscure that he never got paid. And inevitably, Penny and Jenny returned to the Castle. The only person to change permanently was James. Because he alone had actually seen Whipping Jack as he vanished. Giles had had his back turned. Penitentia and Januaria were being coquettish and not looking at him. Frank was trying to free his stooge from police custody. But James looked like he had seen a ghost. Permanently.

·YORK·ROAD·
174

York Road

Where are the others?'

'I think they've forgotten about us,' said the old woman.

'Don't be silly,' replied the man. 'Someone's bound to come down sooner or later. I mean, they can't just leave us here. They'll send a rescue party, or the police, or something.'

'What do you suppose is keeping them? Just you wait 'til I see the manager or whoever's in charge. I'll demand compensation!'

'Compensation?'

'Yes compensation. Me at 81! With my arthritis!'

He stroked his chin. 'Apparently, this place was one of the deepest on the system. But even if the lift's broken down, there should be some stairs.'

'Stairs! You don't think I'm climbing all the way back to the top, do you? It'll take a month of Sundays.'

'Well, if I can find them, I could go up and fetch some help,' he ventured. 'Problem is, I haven't seen any. Perhaps we should take a look around. By the way, I'm Chris.' He held out his hand.

'Irene Potter. Charmed, I'm sure,' she replied. 'And what do you do, when you're not trapped hundreds of feet underground?'

'I'm a tree surgeon,' answered Chris, airily.

'A tree what?' said Irene, a slight note of incredulity creeping into her voice.

'Surgeon,' he said, more distinctly this time. 'I attend to trees that are sick or diseased, or have maybe outgrown their position.'

'Ah, I see. And what, may I ask, brings you down here?'

'Nothing, really. I was with a friend of mine who's a bit of a fanatic about all this,' he waved his hands about. 'When he heard they were opening it to visitors, he persuaded me to come. We were supposed to be going to Kew Gardens afterwards but, well, I don't know now. What about you?'

Irene didn't reply, but instead pointed behind him. 'Do you think we might get over to the other side if we go through there?'

'Maybe,' he replied. 'Shall we investigate?'

'You go on ahead, young man. See what you can find.'

'I'd better take this paraffin lamp with me. The lights only seem to be working in this area.'

'And one of those keeps flickering,' said Irene. 'Have you got a match?'

'Yes.' He lit the lamp. 'There's not much paraffin in this old thing. Wait here, I'll be as quick as I can.'

'Don't you worry about me.'

She watched Chris gradually become enveloped in a haze of yellow light that grew smaller as he disappeared into the passage.

Irene sat alone in the silence. She took in the dark, dank, curved walls of the tunnel. Nearly all the enamelled signs were still intact. Looking up, she could see the thin blue strip that ran the length of the tunnel, the words 'Piccadilly Line' and, below it, the big red roundel with large letters proclaiming this to be 'York Road Station'. On each side of the roundel were advertisements that, though faded and brown at the edges, were still remarkably clear. The Gaumont King's Cross was showing 'Mutiny on the Bounty', starring Clark Gable and Charles Laughton. Forthcoming attractions included Bette Davis in 'Of Human Bondage' and Alfred Hitchcock's 'The Man Who Knew Too Much', with Leslie Banks and Edna Best. At the Hammersmith Palais, Jack Payne and his dance band were performing. Irene's toe began to tap. Then, ever so gently, her body began to sway. She sang, 'I can't give you anything but love, baby. That's the only thing I've plenty of, baby.' Suddenly, the lights went out. She continued. 'It had to be you. It had to be you. I wandered around and finally found somebody who,' Irene's voice grew louder. 'Could make me be true. Could make me be blue.'

'Er... hello?' Chris's voice rang out.

Irene kept on singing. 'And even be glad, just to be sad, thinking of you.'

'Irene, I've found the other platform,' shouted Chris as he made his way back holding the paraffin lamp. Still Irene kept singing. As Chris approached her, his lamp picked out her figure sitting on an upturned sand bucket.

'For nobody else gave me a thrill,' trilled Irene. 'With all your faults I love you still.'

By now, Chris was standing right next to her. She looked up into his face and sang, 'It had to be you, wonderful you. It had to be you.'

He smiled, 'I've found the other platform. Only trouble is, there are a few stairs. We'll have to cross over this railway line. I could carry you.'

She nodded. 'OK then. You carry me and my stick, and I'll carry the lamp. Don't worry, I'm not heavy. I'm four foot two and I weigh four and a half stone. How tall are you?'

'Six foot three,' he replied, bending down to pick her up.

'Ooh, I've not done this since Albert carried me over the threshold of our house in Killick Street in 1939. Now, watch where you're going!'

'Don't worry, I've got you.'

'Well how about a sing-song then?' cried Irene with relish.

'I don't know those old songs from your day,' he said, unenthusiastically.

'Well, what about something more modern then. What about the Kinks?'

'The Kinks?' gasped Chris.

'Yes yes, you know. "Dirty old river, must you keep rolling, flowing into the night." Oh, come on!' she urged.

Chris overcame his embarrassment and joined in. Their voices boomed and echoed around the tunnels.

'As long as I gaze on Waterloo Sunset, I am in paradise,' they sang as they made their way up the steps and through the connecting passages.

'Well, this is the other platform. What now?'

'Oh I am enjoying this,' said Irene. 'Can we go down a bit further?' she asked. 'You see that wooden seat fixed to the wall? Well, there should be another one at the end.'

They moved further down the platform, the swinging lantern picking out the station signs, advertisements and debris on the floor.

'Mind those buckets!' she warned, 'Oh look, there's another lamp. Maybe there's some paraffin in it.'

Chris set Irene down gently and examined the lamp. 'This one's nearly full,' he exclaimed.
'Oh good, now we've both got one. Just a minute, I'll light it.' He handed her the newly lit lantern. She took it and shuffled forward to the stout wooden seat fixed to the tunnel wall. 'It's still here!' she cried.

'What's still here?'

'Look,' said Irene. Chris peered to where Irene's finger was pointing. There, carved in the wood, were the letters I.R. and A.P. surrounded by the shape of a heart.

'My Albert did that,' said Irene. 'We used to meet here when we were courting. I was only sixteen. He wasn't much older. He lived at Finsbury Park. We met here Tuesdays and Fridays to begin with.'

'Why here?' asked Chris.

'Well, he'd been in trouble with the law you see. Nothing serious, mind, but, well, my father would have gone through the roof. He would have stopped me seeing him. Albert had a bit of a reputation. But they were wrong about him. He just needed a bit of love, that's all. Anyway, we kept on meeting here - nearly every day when he was working. Then they closed the station down. Just like that! Well, that was in 1937. We got married two years later, just before the war started.' She sighed. 'This place holds such memories for me. After the war, he worked at Witcomb Cycles in Deptford, making bespoke bicycles - you know, tailored. He made a beautiful one for me. They're still going, you know. Still there, making beautiful bikes...'

'Yes, very interesting I'm sure,' said Chris a little impatiently. 'The thing is, what do we do now? I can't see any way out of here.'

They sat down on the seat together. He pulled a bunch of leaflets out of his coat pocket.

'It says here that there's another old station just a bit to the north of here. Well... it's not a station, exactly. It's one they never completed. They use it for storage now, and there are supposed to be offices there as well.'

Irene looked at him blankly.

'What I mean is,' he continued, 'if we make our way down the track we ought to come across it.'

'You mean we should walk down that tunnel? In the dark?'

'We've got our lanterns,' countered Chris.

'Suppose a train comes. What then?' she asked.

'Don't be silly, this place was shut down years ago. Come on.' He jumped up from the seat, walked to the edge of the platform and lowered himself down onto the railway line. 'It's better than waiting around, anyway.'

Irene made her way to the edge of the platform and looked down at him.

'Perhaps you should go on your own. I'll wait here in case someone...' she paused. 'Oh bother it. I'm too old for this, but very well, help me down.'

Chris reached out and gently lifted her onto the railway track.

'Why don't I give you a piggyback? Come on,' he ordered, and squatted down so that Irene could climb up. She put her arms around his neck and hauled herself up on to his shoulders.

'Just a minute,' she said and leaned over to pick up her lantern.

'Oh yes. Mustn't forget these,' agreed Chris. He rose to his feet with Irene securely attached to his back.

'Lead on, Macduff!' she joked as they made their way into the mouth of the tunnel. For about fifteen minutes they made good progress. Then Irene detected a slowing down.

'Are you getting tired, young man?' she asked.

'No, no. I'm all right,' came the reply.

'Perhaps we should have another sing-song. You know, to cheer us up and keep us going. What about...' she started singing, 'Keep right on to the end of the road, keep right on to the end.'

'Shhhhhh..!' said Chris.

'What's up?'

Chris had stopped and was standing quite still.

'I thought I heard something,' he said.

'I didn't hear anything.'

'You were too busy singing. Anyway, I felt it rather than heard it. Shhhhh...!'

He stood stock-still, listening intently. Irene, still perched on his back, leaned forward slightly, lantern aloft, and peered into the darkness.

They both became aware of a deep rumbling noise, which seemed to be getting louder.

'Saints preserve us!' gasped Irene. 'It's a train!'

Chris didn't move.

'It's a train!' she repeated more urgently. 'Quick turn back.'

'Wha... Wha... What do you mean?' he stammered.

'Behind us,' said Irene. 'It's not far. There was a sort of cubbyhole in the wall. It's about the same height as the platform. There's room for both of us, I think.'

Chris didn't move or say anything. Irene wriggled about on his back.

'Come on,' she urged. 'What's the matter? Come on or we're done for!'

'But the rail!' Chris cried. 'That rail three feet away from us. It must be live! It could kill both of us if I touch it.'

'Well don't touch it!' she ordered. 'Look, come on!'

At last, Chris got the message and turned round to retrace his steps. The noise of the train was getting louder.

'Can't you go a bit faster?' cried Irene.

'I'll try,' he said, starting a peculiar sort of jog along the track. His lantern swung about uncontrollably and Irene bounced up and down on his back, holding her lantern high and shrieking,

'Here it is!' she cried at last.

Chris pulled up with a start and sure enough, there was the alcove. The opening was at just the right level for Irene to alight and ease herself against the back wall. He climbed up to join her.

'The noise seems to have stopped,' observed Irene. She pushed Chris out of the way so she could get a good view down the tunnel. 'Oh, it hasn't stopped. It's just going very slowly. I can see it now.'

'Perhaps we should wave our lanterns about.'

'Don't be silly,' retorted Irene. 'They might go out. Lets wait 'til it gets a bit nearer. Then, you hold me round the waist and I'll lean out and get their attention.'

Slowly, the train drew nearer. Irene could make out the driver's cab and what looked like two figures. Eventually, the train stopped about twenty-five yards away from them. The figures were standing facing each other on either side of the cab, and the centre door leading into the passenger compartment behind them was open. The compartment was brightly lit and Irene and Chris could see several people inside. Chris was now crouched down, looking over Irene's shoulder.

'It must be one of those enthusiast trains,' he whispered into her ear. 'You know, one of those special trains that takes railway enthusiasts around old disused stations,' he said.

'Oh, I see,' murmured Irene. 'Why are you whispering?'

With a loud 'clank,' the train began to move forward very slowly.

'Pass me my stick,' said Irene. 'I'll rap on the window as he goes past.'

The train drew closer and closer. Then, miraculously, just as the cab drew level with them, it stopped. Irene seized her opportunity. She rapped loudly on the window of the cab. The two men turned and looked in amazement at the solitary figure of Chris, crouching in the refuge and swinging his lantern.

Notes on the Stories:

The zoo in Walworth was a huge affair running from Manor Place to Kennington Park Road and covered rather well in issue Nine of Smoke magazine. Though you'd have to look in the March 14th 2004 issue of the Sunday Times to find a full depiction of the world where the Inuit live after their death. It's in a Heaven far beyond the Christian one apparently. Details about the appearance of Ikiyana at the pleasure garden are indeed verifyable through the British Library though it's unclear whether her family made a habit of visiting other recreational spots like Cremorne or Vauxhall.

On matters of pleasure and pain in the early Victorian period a book appeared by the pseudonymous author Pisanus Fraxi called The Index of Forbidden Books. The title was a parody of the Vatican's list of books Catholics are forbidden to read, what it actually was a review of every item in the author's collection of pornography. Pisanus Fraxi has been tentatively identified as "Walter" whose "My Secret Life" has become a classic of Victorian porn and began the craze for producing Victorian porn in the early 1970s at a time when the Obscene Publications Squad cracked down on any written description of heterosexual anal sex unless it was old enough to be considered of historical importance. In the Index, Fraxi/Walter includes a description of a pamphlet concerning "Whipping Jack", a figure that terrified women in London in the late 18th century. He would appear from nowhere and whip women's buttocks before disappearing again.

Scott was perhaps having a bit of a laugh with the idea of alien memory transfer pills though something has to account for the strange nights in Brixton and attendant memory loss that I'm sure we've all experienced. Atlantic Road is the opening part of a journey of discovery and revelation undertaken by the narrator that carries on into Coldharbour Lane in the next edition and finishes in Lewisham Way.

What is perhaps most disturbing about the Dead Woods Song is its lack of specific place. It could be any bit of metropolitan woodland from Osterley to Epping, Abbey Wood to Richmond. Those interested in the prequel to Dead Woods Song can find it on the F&M website but, ahem, parental guidance is advised.

Finally York Road is one of the unused stations on the underground which also includes the British Museum (haunted by a screaming queen) and Aldwych by a ghost that used to haunt the Royal Strand Theatre above. As far as we are aware though there are more ghost stations without a ghost than with.

Pictures of tree in Dead Woods Song is of the Hardy Tree in Old St Pancras Churchyard. This tree got it's name from the poet and writer Thomas Hardy who studied architecture and was charged with moving graves and coffins out of the route of the tracks running into St Pancras. One story goes that a coffin broke open in front of the sensitive West Country lad and his appalled reaction to this was one of his first published poems. The gravestones Hardy moved are bunched around a solitary tree rather in the fashion of a chocolate orange. The photo on this page also comes from St Pancras graveyard and is the tomb of Sir John Soames. The shape of which apparently inspired the design of the traditional red telephone box.

SUBSCRIBE

To this year's One Eye Grey for £9.00 and get a free mystery book (NB this is the same mystery book as last year!). Meanwhile the collected 2007 One Eye Grey is available for £7.00 including postage or you could go for our Book Club Special which gets you five copies of all three of last years One Eyes for £25.00. Bargain! See website for details.

CONTRIBUTE

F and M Publications welcomes contributions of short stories based on folktales or ghost stories or even just weird tales with a London setting. Be creative be playful, be horrible but be London. Stories (up to 2,500 words) should be e-mailed to penny@fandmpublications.co.uk
Please attach the text as a Rich Text or Plain Text file.
More details at **www.fandmpublications.co.uk**

ADVERTISING

One Eye Grey does not sell advertising in the traditional sense but does welcome payment for sentences or paragraphs which may or may not contain positive references to the sponsor's product, depending on the mood of our whimsical ethical advertising committee. So you could stump up for a favourable mention of your product in some dialogue by a nice character, shell out for a positive endorsement of rival's merchandise by a bad person or even cough up for a paragraph discussion of virtues of your goods or services etc.

At the end of One Eye Grey there will be an acknowledgment of your kind donation with a phrase along the lines of: Sentence three, paragraph two, page seventeen was kindly brought to you by the Japanese Whaling Commission. Be creative and make us an offer through **OneeyeGrey@fandmpublications.co.uk**